Listen, Said the Donkey

Tales of the First Christmas

Story by
Jean Little

Illustrations by
Werner Zimmermann

North Winds Press
An Imprint of Scholastic Canada Ltd.

The paintings for this book were created in watercolour and pencil
on Arches Watercolour Paper.

The display type in this book was set in DeVinne
and the text type was set in Bookman Light Italic and ITC Caslon Book.

Library and Archives Canada Cataloguing in Publication

Little, Jean, 1932-
Listen, said the donkey : tales of the first Christmas / Jean Little ;
Werner Zimmermann, illustrator.

ISBN 0-439-95782-6

1. Jesus Christ — Nativity — Juvenile fiction. I. Zimmermann, Werner II. Title.

PS8523.I77L53 2006   jC813'.54   C2006-901157-5

6 5 4 3 2 1   Printed in Canada   06 07 08 09 10

To Margie Mackay, with my love.

— J.L.

To the memory of my mother Katharina and the stories she told us in childhood.

— W.Z.

In the Stable

There was room in the inn at last. A serving girl came to the tumbledown stable to get Mary and Joseph and their baby.

When the door closed behind them, a donkey, a lamb, a cat and a tiny white dog stretched and stirred. An old camel looked in at the high window.

For days they had listened to Mary and Joseph talking and the baby crying or gurgling. But now all was still.

The lamb broke the hush. "I miss the baby," she said.

"So do I," said the cat.

"Listen," said the donkey. "A story may help. Let's all tell about what brought us here the night the baby was born."

"Good," said the lamb. "I love stories."

"I should go first," the camel announced. "I have travelled farthest and I am by far the most important animal here."

The cat's fur stood up until she looked enormous. Her golden eyes glinted. "The donkey was the first one here," she said, "and it was his idea. He will begin."

"Go ahead, donkey," said the small dog. "We're listening."

The cat stalked over to the manger and stretched out. The lamb snuggled down in the hay. The dog stayed curled in a shadowy corner. The camel snorted but he remained at the window.

And the donkey began.

The
Donkey's Tale

*Once I was always hungry. When I looked in my
manger, there was never enough hay. When I looked in
my water pail, it was empty.*

"I'd have stolen food," said the cat.
"I'd have run away," whispered the dog.
"I hope the story gets better," grunted the camel.

*I was tied up and could not run away. My master
never let me rest. He beat me. "Work harder!" he shouted.
"Go faster!" But no matter how hard I worked or how fast
I went, he would hit me again and again.*

"Some people are cruel," the dog said with a shiver.

*One day my master wanted me to go up a steep hill.
But my load was too heavy, so I stood still. He whipped
me until I nearly fell, but I could not carry that load.*

"What made him stop?" growled the cat.

A man and woman were passing. "Joseph, we need a donkey," the woman said.

"We do," said he, "but not this donkey, Mary. He is far too thin."

"I will make him fat," she said.

"Look at him. He is sick," said the man.

"I will make him well," she said. "Buy him, Joseph. He will be our friend."

"My master would never sell *me*," boasted the camel. The cat stared up at him. The tip of her tail twitched.

When my master had Mary and Joseph's money, he told them they were fools. "That donkey will be dead in a week," he said. But Joseph and Mary took me to a warm, dry stable where I soon grew well and strong. They saved my life.

"Is that the end?" asked the lamb.

"Hush," said the cat. "What happened next, donkey?"

Joseph prepared to go on a journey. In my saddlebags he put food and soft cloth. I carried Mary on my back much of the way, since her baby was soon to be born.

"Our baby?" asked the dog.

"Our baby," said the donkey. After a moment, he went on.

When we set out, the road was full of travellers. We went slowly for Mary's sake. It was very late when we got here. We asked at every inn in town, but there was no room.

"Poor Mary," said the lamb.

Joseph was so worried. At last he found a woman who let us sleep in this old stable. Mary had her baby right here on the hay.

At first the stable was warm. They wrapped the baby in the cloth from my saddlebag. And they made him a bed in the manger.

Then visitors began to come — shepherds and villagers, kings and angels. Mary grew weary. When the visitors left and she slept at last, Joseph meant to keep watch. But he was so tired that he fell asleep.

While Joseph slept, I stayed awake. At dawn, a bitter wind came up. I saw the baby shivering with cold. So I blew my warm breath on him and covered him with more hay. At last, the cold woke Joseph. He hurried to the manger. Then he smiled at me.

"You kept him warm," he said. "Mary was right. You are our friend. And you have saved the life of a king."

"He *is* a king," said the lamb. "The angels said so. They said, 'He will be a saviour to all the sheep.' He's not just any baby."

"It wasn't *angels*," snorted the camel. "Trust a lamb to get it wrong."

"I would have done it for any baby," said the donkey softly. "I know how it feels to be cold."

Everyone was quiet for a moment. Then the cat said gently, "It is your turn now, lamb."

And so she began.

The
Lamb's Tale

I was still very young on the night of the angels.

"I tell you, it wasn't *angels*," said the camel. "It was a new star."

"No," said the lamb. "The whole sky went white. There were shining wings, and singing. It was angels."

"Go on, lamb," said the cat, flicking her tail and glancing at the camel.

The angels told us to go to the stable. They said, "You will find a baby lying in a manger. And he will be a saviour to all the sheep."

"I think you have that bit wrong, my lamb," said the cat.

The camel sniffed. But he did not speak.

The shepherds ran to the stable. My shepherd boy picked me up and ran after them, all the way here. We saw people give gifts. A king went in just ahead of us. He gave the baby gold!

Then my boy stepped forward and set me next to the baby. "A ewe lamb is as fine as gold," he said.

"Will Mary and Joseph keep you?" the dog asked from his dark corner.

"I think they might give me back to the boy," said the lamb. "I'd like that. He's a kind boy. And he loves me."

"It must be good to be loved," said the little dog.

"My star was better than angels," said the camel. "If you are quite through, lamb, I think it is my turn."

The cat's eyes gleamed. "This should be good," she said.

And so the camel began.

The
Camel's Tale

"My home is far to the east — "

"What's 'east'?" asked the lamb.

"You would not understand if I told you," snapped the camel. "Just listen."

The little lamb hung her head. "I'm sorry," she said.

The cat hissed. Then she walked over to the lamb. "Ask him another question," she said. "Ask him why he stayed behind when the kings left."

The lamb looked up at the camel. But before she could speak, the camel rushed on.

Melchior, my master, is very rich. He lives in a great palace. He and his two friends are incredibly wise. They study the stars. One night, I heard him shout, "I see a new star. It is so big and so bright. I have never seen such a star before."

Then his friends rushed in. They shouted too.
"We must go where the star leads," they all said.
"It must mean the birth of a great king."

"How do you know what they said?" asked the cat
softly. "I did not know camels lived inside palaces."
The camel looked down his nose at her. "I hear
things," he said coldly. Then he went on with his story.

They got ready for a journey. They packed food and
tents. But they took much more. Rich gifts. I myself
carried the gold. It was the best gift. I was chosen
because I am the best camel. We set out in a great
caravan to find the new king.

"How did you know where to look?" asked the dog.
"I am coming to that," said the camel.

It took weeks. We followed that star, so we went
by night. It shone with a great, white fire.

I thought the star would lead us to the big city, but the ruler there had not heard of a new king. So we journeyed on until we came to this place. Here, Melchior and his friends gave their gifts to this child. I still do not understand why. How could a king be born here? *This is no royal birthplace. These people are not the best people.*

"They are the best in the world," the donkey said hotly.

"The angels told the shepherds they would find the baby lying in a manger," the lamb said. "And they did."

"Those wise men of yours left their rich gifts here," said the cat. "Even your fine gold. Were they fools, old camel?"

"Even wise men make mistakes," said the camel. But for the first time, he sounded uncertain.

"Wait until you hear *my* story," the cat said. "Listen well, old camel."

And so the cat began.

The
Cat's Tale

My master lived in a palace. He was wise. He studied the stars. But even wise men can have foolish camels. My master's old camel was the silliest camel in Persia.

"What?" shouted the camel. "Don't listen to her. She's only a cat. How dare she!"

"I am a Persian cat," said the cat, "and my master's name was . . . Melchior."

Everyone looked at the old camel. His head drooped. The stable was so quiet you could have heard a mouse sneeze.

I was in the room when my master first beheld that star. I was washing my whiskers, so I wasn't paying attention. Whiskers are hard to get right. But he rushed over to me and held me up in the air. "The star — it must mean a new king," he shouted. "We will go and find him."

I was bored. Palaces are not much fun. So I went along.

Melchior rode on his strong young camel. He kept me inside his robe because it was cold. I am a very fine cat.

The dog and lamb and donkey nodded. She was indeed a fine cat.

The camel sniffed again. But not loudly.

We'd have been here sooner if it weren't for this old camel. He took us down the wrong road. My master was dozing and did not notice, so we went all the way to that other city.

We should not have gone there — for that king, Herod, is a bad man. A jealous man. He does not even have a cat. We left Herod's city and came here. This camel did not carry the gold — he carried tents. He's only a pack animal and he is old and lame. He was left here to be sold.

When the cat finished, nobody spoke for a moment.

"Why are you still here, cat?" the lamb asked at last.

"I go where I choose," said the cat. "I like this baby. I make him smile. Melchior wanted me to return with him, but I stayed. I am wiser than he."

"Your new master is a baby," grunted the camel. "I suppose you think *he* is wise."

"All kittens start out wise," said the cat. "And this one is a king. He may stay wise even when he becomes a man. Now, pup, let's hear your story."

The small dog stayed hiding in his corner. "I am afraid to tell it," he whispered. "I would need to trust you." He looked up at the window.

The old camel sighed. "You can trust me, pup. I may be sad and silly, sometimes, but I am not bad. I wanted someone to look up to me, that's all."

"Then I will trust you," the dog said. "But if someone comes, don't tell them I am here."

The animals settled down for the last story.

The Dog's Tale

I ran away the night we arrived. My mistress is a rich man's wife. She is going to visit her mother. We stopped here because my mistress grew ill.

She does not let me run free. Ever. She keeps me in a cage or on her lap. When I displease her, she strikes me.

On our first night here, my mistress was so angry she threw me across the room. The inn door was open and I fled into the night.

The master shouted that I was worth a lot of money and ordered his wife's servant to find me. But the servant is my friend. "Good luck, pup," she said when she caught up with me. "Away with you." She told the master that I could not be found.

But he offered a reward to anyone who would bring me back. So the stable boy keeps looking for me.

"Maybe your mistress will give up the search," the donkey said gently.

"Maybe," said the little dog, "for she does not love me. She keeps me only to show off — not many have dogs like me.

"My mistress is vain and she is cruel. I will never go back to her. I am very hungry out here, but I have made up my mind. I would rather die than go back."

"But Mary and Joseph don't know why you're hiding," said the lamb. "They might give away where you are."

"They have never seen me tucked away in my corner," the dog said. "Only the baby knows I am here. He is such a fine baby. I can make him smile too, cat. I have never loved anyone before, but I do love our baby. I would do anything for him."

The
Christmas Tale

The stable door opened. The little dog shrank back into the shadows. But it was only Mary and Joseph.

"Are you sure we must leave?" Mary whispered.

"We are in great danger," Joseph said. "The angel in my dream told me we must take the child and flee into Egypt. Herod searches for us!"

Silently, the animals watched Joseph load the saddlebags onto the donkey. In Mary's arms, their baby slept.

"It's a long way," the camel whispered. "The child might grow cold."

"But didn't you say that he's not one of the best babies?" the cat purred.

"I didn't mean it," said the camel. "Forgive me, cat. I know now that he must be a king. Or a saviour to all the sheep. Isn't that what your angels said, lamb?"

She nodded.

"I'll go with them," said the cat. "They'll need me to show them the way. Besides, they worship cats in Egypt. Lead on, my donkey friend." Like smoke, she drifted after them.

Joseph led the donkey out into the quiet night.

"Where are you off to, sir?" the stable boy asked.

"We must go home now," Joseph said. "We cannot take the lamb with us. Would you see that she gets back to her shepherd?"

The camel turned his head to watch them go. The lamb snuggled down to wait. The dog stayed hidden.

The stable boy was talking to himself. "If they're going back to Nazareth, then why did they go south, not north?"

When he was gone, the camel asked, "Why didn't you go with them, dog? You could have left before your people woke up. You could have been free."

"I . . . I think I am meant to stay a little longer," the dog said.

The day was half over when soldiers arrived. "Was a baby born here?" a rough voice asked. "King Herod sent us to find him."

"Yes, one was born here," said the boy, "but his family has gone. They were from Nazareth. They said they were going home, but — "

Suddenly the small dog ran out into the yard.

"The missing dog!" the boy shouted. "I must catch him and get the reward!"

The dog ducked behind a cart, then dashed out again, turned the other way, and cut down an alley. The boy raced after him.

"Nazareth, is it?" said the soldier. "Well, they can't have gone far. After them! King Herod wants that child!" He led his soldiers north.

When the stable boy finally caught the dog, he brought him to the rich woman and was paid his reward.

Later that day the woman and her husband rode away, with her servant carrying the dog in a cage.

Through the bars, the servant rubbed the dog's ears. "You're a brave boy," she said. His feathery tail waved in response.

"Why didn't he stay hidden?" asked the lamb. "He feared his mistress so. He must have known the stable boy would catch him."

"Yes. He must have known," said the camel. He cleared his throat. "He made the soldiers go the wrong way, you see. North — not south, where our baby is. By the time they realize their mistake and come back, the baby should be safe. If he is, the dog will have his wish."

"But he'll never *know*," said the lamb. "Maybe he saved the baby, but maybe not. And he'll never know."

"I don't think he will mind not knowing," said the old camel. His voice held wonder.

Just then the shepherd boy arrived to carry the lamb away. As they set off, the camel called after her, "I was wrong, lamb. You really did see angels."

"I know," called the lamb. "Goodbye, old camel."

The camel watched until the lamb was out of sight. Then he bowed his head to take a last look inside the empty stable.

But it was not quite empty. A tiny mouse was staring up at him. "I am glad that cat is finally gone," the mouse said. "What was it you were all talking about?"

"Listen," said the camel. "Listen, mouse. I have stories to tell you."